KU-161-865

The Two Stubborn Pirates

by Oakley Graham

Licensed exclusively to Top That Publishing Ltd
Tide Mill Way, Woodbridge, Suffolk, IP12 1AP, UK
www.topthatpublishing.com
Copyright © 2013 Tide Mill Media
All rights reserved
2 4 6 8 9 7 5 3 1
Manufactured in China

Written by Oakley Graham
Illustrated by Kimberley Scott

All rights reserved. No part of this publication may be reproduced, stored in a retrieval system, or transmitted in any form or by any means, electronic, mechanical, photocopying, recording or otherwise, without the prior written permission of the publisher. Neither this book nor any part or any of the illustrations, photographs or reproductions contained in it shall be sold or disposed of otherwise than as a complete book, and any unauthorised sale of such part illustration, photograph or reproduction shall be deemed to be a breach of the publisher's copyright.

ISBN 978-1-78244-220-2

A catalogue record for this book is available from the British Library

'For my own stubborn little pirates, Noah and Oakie.'
Oakley Graham

On their ships' masts were black flags as dark as the grave,
Striking fear and terror as they sailed through the waves.

This is the tale of two stubborn pirates who just didn't get on,
And their fight is remembered in this pirate shanty song.

And it's down, down, sink them all down!

Bluebeard owned a map which led to lots of pirate treasure;
More than enough gold and jewels for a life full of pleasure.

Crafty Redbeard stole the map in the dead of the night,
So Bluebeard set sail after him, determined to fight!

And it's down, down, sink them all down!

'Clear the decks!' fearsome Bluebeard declared;
'Get the boarding-axe sharpened, the cutlasses bared!

Set the cannons ready,
and then quickly bring to me,
The fuse for the cannons,
and the powder-room key!'

And it's down, down,
sink them all down!

Bluebeard's ship was closing in as
Redbeard battled against the tide.
'We'll blow them all to smithereens!
There's nowhere for them to hide!'

For the two stubborn pirates
this really wasn't a game.
Bluebeard ordered his pirates
to get ready and take aim!

And it's down, down, sink them all down!

'Open the hatches, light the fuses and away with the faint-hearted.' Bluebeard's fearsome pirate crew prepared to get the battle started!

Pirates loaded the cannons in the gloomy darkness below deck,
While Bluebeard poked and prodded an angry boil on his neck.

Redbeard sensed he was in danger and made a starboard turn,
As cannonballs flew through the air and whistled past the stern.

And it's down, down, sink them all down!

Side by side the ships sailed; both crews calling their war cry,
As the stubborn pirates stood on deck, their cutlasses held high.

And it's down, down,
sink them all down!

'I want my treasure map back!' angry Bluebeard declared.
Redbeard cried, 'Come and get it, unless you're too scared!'

And it's down, down,
sink them all down!

The pirates fought day and night, until both ships were alight.
And when the ships began to sink, they continued with their fight.

And it's down, down, sink them all down!

On their ships' masts were black flags as dark as the grave,
Striking fear and terror as they sailed through the waves.
This is the tale of two stubborn pirates who just didn't get on.

Down in Davy Jones' locker, their fight still carries on …

... and it's down, down, sink them all down!

N
E
W
S